Stuck
at the
Top

written by Jay Dale

illustrated by Craig Smith

Cam and Granny were
on the big wheel.
Round and round they went.

"Look at me!" shouted Cam.
"I'm way up here!"

Mum waved from down on the ground.
The big wheel went round and round.

"Granny!" shouted Cam.
"Are you having fun?"

"Yes," said Granny.

But she didn't look like
she was having fun.
She looked scared.

"Look!" shouted Cam.
"We are right at the top.
I can see all the way to the sea."

Just then, there was an enormous
BANG, a big **CRUNCH**
and an enormous
SCREEEEECHHH!!

The big wheel stopped.
Cam and Granny were stuck
right at the top!

"Yippee!" shouted Cam.
"We are stuck right at the top!"

"Oh, no!" cried Granny,
taking a careful look over the side.
"It's a long way down."

Cam turned and looked, too.
He could see Mum down on the ground.
She looked like a little ant.

7

"WOW!" shouted Cam.
"It's so much fun up here!"
And with that,
he began to swing his seat
up and down.

"Cam!" cried Granny,
going white with fright.
"Please stop!
I'm scared and I want to come down."

"I'm sorry," said Cam.
"I'll come and sit beside you
and hold your hand."

"No!" cried Granny.
"Stay where you are!
You can't sit beside me.
You need to sit still.
The seat could tip back."

So Cam sat as still as he could.

Just then, there was
an enormous **BOOM**,
a big **BRUMMMM**
and an enormous
CHUG! CHUG! CHUG!

The big wheel began to move.

"Oh, no!" cried Cam.
"We are going down."

"At last!" said Granny.
"That's one ride I will never EVER forget!"

"Me, too!" smiled Cam.

When Cam and Granny got down,
a nice man helped Granny
off the big wheel.

Mum came over and gave them both
a big hug.

"Was it scary at the top?" she asked Cam.

"No!" laughed Cam.
"It was lots of fun.
Can Granny and I go on again?"

Mum and Cam turned around
to look for Granny.
But she had gone!